Ian Whybrow   Ed Eave

Say Hello
to the
Snowy Animals!

Sandy Creek

Come with me and say hello
in the land of ice and snow.

Who's that fishing over there?
Say hello to the polar bear.

Hello, Polar Bear!

Grrrr, grrrr, grrrr!

Here's a funny feathery fowl!
Say hello to the snowy owl.

Hello, Snowy Owl!

Hoo-hoo, hoo-hoo!

Caribou huffs and stamps through the storm.
His thick brown coat will keep him warm.

Hello, Caribou!

Huff, huff, huff!

Out to sea, I spy a whale
spouting water and splashing his tail.

Sliding's fun for a fat little seal,
but think how cold your tummy would feel!

Hello, Seal!
Honk, honk, honk!

Puffin, with your stripy bill,
eat those fish, or your friends soon will!

Arctic hares can jump and race.
Look out! Husky loves to chase!

Hello, Arctic Hare!

Thump,
thump,
thump!

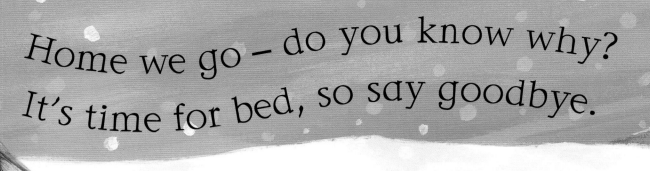

Home we go – do you know why?
It's time for bed, so say goodbye.

Goodbye, Polar Bear!
Grrrr, grrrr, grrrr!

Goodbye, Caribou!
Huff, huff, huff!

Goodbye, Snowy Owl!
Hoo-hoo, hoo-hoo!

Goodbye, Puffin!
Flap, flap, flap!

Goodbye, Whale!
Swish-swash, swish-swash!

Goodbye, Seal!
Honk, honk, honk!

Goodbye, Arctic Hare!
Thump, thump, thump!

What a lovely snowy night!
Goodbye, Husky! Snuggle up tight.

For Sophia
and Amélie – I.W.

For Jack
and Ralphie – E.E.

Text copyright © 2007 by Ian Whybrow
Illustrations copyright © 2007 by Edward Eaves
Moral rights asserted.

This 2008 edition published by Sandy Creek
by arrangement with Macmillan Publishers Ltd.

ISBN: 978-0-7607-9675-7

Printed and bound in China

5 7 9 10 8 6

First published 2007 by Macmillan Children's Books
a division of Macmillan Publishers Ltd.